Dear Parents, Caregivers, and Educators:

It is with great pleasure that Nationwide's Make Safe Happen program and Safe Kids Worldwide present *Clifford Takes a Swim*! This story for beginning readers teaches children about water safety as they join Clifford the Big Red Dog, Emily Elizabeth, and their friends on a day full of fun at the town pool.

Swimming is one of the most important skills for kids to learn. It helps keep them safe in and around water, and it's a lot of fun, too!

So before you and your child head out for the pool, take a fun adventure with Clifford and his friends and read this story together. We also encourage you to visit www.safekids.org/water to download your own Water Watcher card so you'll be ready for your next visit to the pool.

Our hope is that you and your child will use this book as an opportunity to discuss these very important water safety tips together, and have a great time making a big splash.

Sincerely,

Your friends at Nationwide and Safe Kids Worldwide

Clifford
Takes a Swim

Norman Bridwell

The Bridwells would like to thank Frank Rocco for his contributions to this book.

For information regarding permission, write to Scholastic Inc., Attention: Permissions Department, 557 Broadway, New York, NY 10012.

This book is a work of fiction. Names, characters, places, and incidents are either the product of the author's imagination or are used fictitiously, and any resemblance to actual persons, living or dead, business establishments, events, or locales is entirely coincidental.

ISBN 978-1-338-08716-1

10 9 8 7 6 5 4 3 2   16 17 18 19 20

Printed in the U.S.A.   40

First printing 2016

SCHOLASTIC INC.

Hi! I'm Emily Elizabeth, and this is my dog, Clifford. Today we are going to the town pool with my parents. I've been taking swim lessons, and today all the families are coming to see what we've learned.

We are going to show them how we follow the pool rules — no diving, running, or rough play — and that we can get into the pool safely, float, go underwater, and swim all the way across the pool! Then we're having a big barbeque to celebrate.

My class meets Coach Carole on the pool deck. We learned to only go in the pool when an adult is watching us.

"Okay, ready?" Coach says. "Everybody in!"

We get into the pool with our feet first, just like we were taught.

"Great job!" Coach says. "Now let's show everyone how you learned to float."

The lifeguard, Samir, is watching us, too. He gives us a thumbs-up!

"Welcome, parents!" Coach Carole says. "Today, your kids will play in the Dolphin Games to demonstrate what they have learned in swim class. Of course, they'll have some fun, too!"

Coach Carole went on to explain that we would each get a dolphin pin for our hard work.

I'm so excited for my parents and Clifford to see me swim!

We split up into teams for the first game. It's water basketball!

"Children, while you're playing, show how you can bob in the water," says Coach Carole. "And also how you can push off from the bottom of the pool to jump up and make a shot!"

My friends and I toss the ball around to each other. Everyone is jumping and laughing and splashing. When it's my turn, I imagine I'm a dolphin. I soar out of the water and shoot the ball.

Score!

During the basketball game, Lisa accidentally throws the ball out of the pool. Clifford dashes across the pool deck to fetch it. Uh-oh!

4FT

3FT

"Clifford!" I cry out. "There's no running by the pool — it's not safe."

Clifford already knows how to swim, but he doesn't know the pool rules like I do. I have to make sure to keep him safe by telling him what I learned in our lessons.

The next game is an underwater treasure hunt where we get to show off how well we can swim underwater! Coach Carole has hidden five gems and five gold coins somewhere in the pool and we have to find them.

"Ready, set, hunt!" Coach Carole says.

As I go underwater, I imagine that I'm a mermaid looking for lost treasure. Just then I spot a golden coin!

Suddenly, Clifford dives into the pool! I think he wants to help find the treasure, too.

"Clifford!" I shout. "There's no diving or rough play in the pool."

He swims over and licks my face. That means he's sorry.

The final game is a relay. This will show that we can swim across the pool.

When it's my turn, I kick my feet hard and breathe just as I was taught. When I turn my head to the side for air, I can hear my classmates cheering, "Go, Emily Elizabeth, go!"

When I finish my lap and get out of the pool, my classmate Ginny says, "You did such a great job. But I'm nervous. What if I can't swim the whole way?"

"You can do it, Ginny!" I say. "I've seen you do it so many times before in class."

"You're right," Ginny says, feeling better. "I *can* do it!"

Ginny gets a surprise when she gets into the pool. Clifford gets in and dog-paddles right next to her!

With Clifford by her side, she feels even better about swimming across the pool.

Finally, it's time for the barbeque celebration. After all that hard work, I'm hungry.

"Congratulations, children!" Coach Carole announces, then hands out our pins. "You've all learned so much in your swim lessons. I'm very proud of you.

"Before we finish, I have one more pin to give out. It's for a swimmer who learned all the pool rules *and* showed kindness to a friend who needed help. That special swimmer is . . . Clifford!"

Coach puts a dolphin pin on Clifford's collar and then gives him a tasty bone.

SHALLOW WATER
NO DIVING
RUNNING
ROUGH PLAY

Later, all the kids from my lessons go back into the pool to play. This time our parents come with us!

Since Coach Carole had to leave for the day, my mom volunteers to be the Water Watcher for the kids in my class.

That means that she wears a special card around her neck and promises to look out for us at all times. I'm so proud that my mom is helping out!

Clifford comes in the water with us, too! He floats on his back like a big red raft and we climb aboard. I love swimming with Clifford!